BEN 10™

AND THEN THERE WERE 10 AND THE KRAKKEN

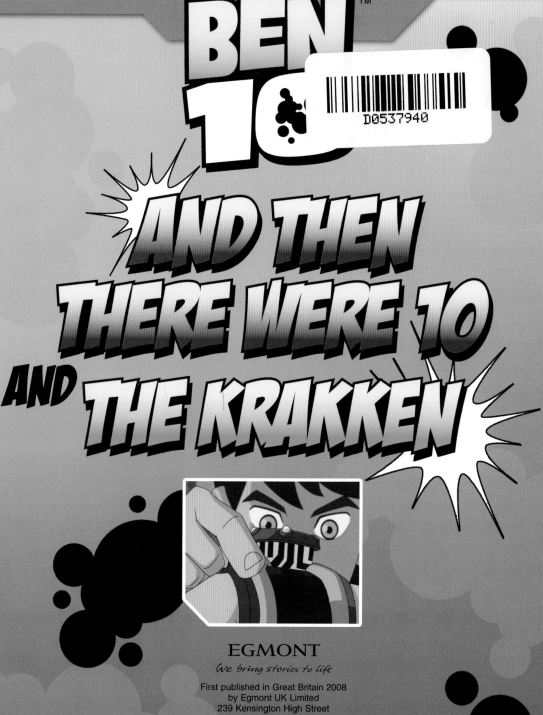

EGMONT
We bring stories to life

First published in Great Britain 2008
by Egmont UK Limited
239 Kensington High Street
London W8 6SA

Ben 10 and all related characters and elements
are trademarks of and © Cartoon Network.
(s08)

ISBN 978 1 4052 4165 6
5 7 9 10 8 6 4

Printed in Italy

BEN 10™

AND THEN THERE WERE 10

BEN TENNYSON IS A 10-YEAR-OLD KID WHO'S JUST FINISHED SCHOOL FOR THE SUMMER. HE'S OFF ON A ROAD TRIP WITH HIS GRANDPA MAX IN THEIR OLD 'RV' – THE RUSTBUCKET! MEANWHILE, STRANGE THINGS ARE HAPPENING IN OUTER SPACE.

AN ALIEN SPACESHIP IS CRUISING SILENTLY THROUGH SPACE WHEN SUDDENLY, *BOOM!* A SMALLER SHIP DELIVERS A DEVASTATING BLAST OF ENERGY!

POW!!

ZAP! POW! THE ATTACK CONTINUES, ROCKING THE BIGGER SPACE CRAFT.

ON BOARD THE DAMAGED SHIP IS THE MONSTROUS-LOOKING VILGAX, AN EVIL ALIEN WARLORD.

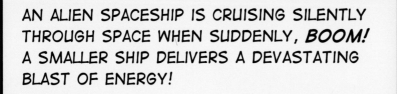

ZAP!

I HAVE COME TOO FAR TO BE DENIED.

THE OMNITRIX SHALL BE MINE, AND THERE IS NOT A BEING IN THE GALAXY WHO DARES STAND IN MY WAY!

THE SPACE CHASE CONTINUES ...

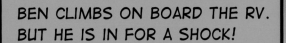

BEN CLIMBS ON BOARD THE RV. BUT HE IS IN FOR A SHOCK!

WHAT IS *SHE* DOING HERE?

IT'S HIS COUSIN, GWEN.

TAKE IT EASY DWEEB, THIS WASN'T MY IDEA. SOMEONE CONVINCED MY MUM THAT GOING CAMPING FOR THE SUMMER WOULD BE GOOD FOR ME.

I THOUGHT IT WOULD BE FUN IF YOUR COUSIN JOINED US THIS SUMMER, IS THAT A PROBLEM?

"I CAN'T BELIEVE IT, I WAIT ALL SCHOOL YEAR TO GO ON THIS TRIP, AND NOW THE QUEEN OF COOTIES IS ALONG FOR THE RIDE!" MOANS BEN.

IT'S ALMOST DARK BY THE TIME THEY GET TO THE CAMPSITE. MAX QUICKLY FIXES UP SOME DINNER.

"CHOW TIME!" SAYS MAX. "MARINATED MEAL WORMS. IT'S HARD TO FIND THEM FRESH. THEY'RE A DELICACY IN SOME COUNTRIES."

AND TOTALLY GROSS IN OTHERS!

URGH, COULDN'T WE JUST HAVE A BURGER OR SOMETHING?

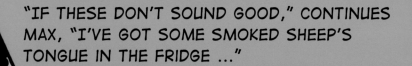

"IF THESE DON'T SOUND GOOD," CONTINUES MAX, "I'VE GOT SOME SMOKED SHEEP'S TONGUE IN THE FRIDGE ..."

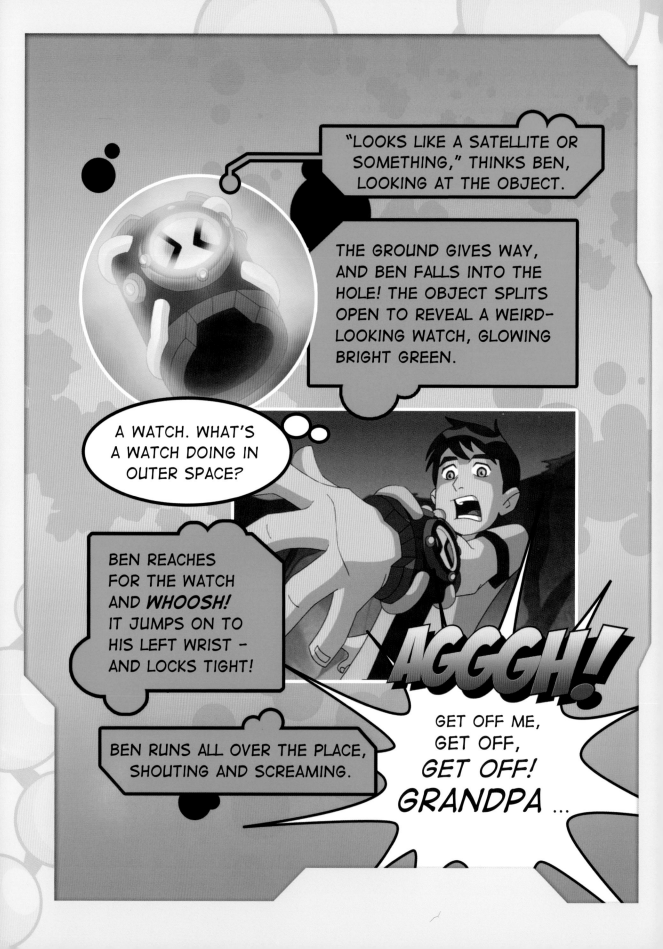

BACK IN THE FOREST, BEN PULLS HIMSELF OUT OF THE CRATER. HE TRIES AGAIN TO GET THE WATCH OFF, BUT NOTHING WORKS.

BEN TAKES A CLOSE LOOK AT THE WATCH AND PRESSES A BUTTON. IT POPS UP AND BLINKS GREEN. A PICTURE OF A MONSTER SUDDENLY APPEARS.

COOL!

BEN CAN'T RESIST PRESSING THE BUTTON.

... AND SUDDENLY BEN HAS TRANSFORMED INTO A BURNING MAN – *HEATBLAST!* HE RUNS THROUGH THE FOREST CRYING OUT IN TERROR.

AGGGH!

I'M ON FIRE, I'M ON FIRE ... HEY, I'M ON FIRE, AND I'M OK. CHECK IT OUT, *I'M TOTALLY HOT!*

BEN TRIES OUT HIS NEW POWERS – IT'S PRETTY COOL BEING ABLE TO SHOOT *FIREBALLS!* BUT IT ISN'T LONG BEFORE HE ACCIDENTALLY SETS FIRE TO SOME TREES. THE FIRE SPREADS AND SOON A HUGE FOREST FIRE IS RAGING! HEATBLAST PANICS.

JUST THEN, MAX AND GWEN APPEAR, ARMED WITH FIRE EXTINGUISHERS. BUT THEY DIDN'T RECKON ON FINDING BEN DISGUISED AS A MONSTER FIREBALL!

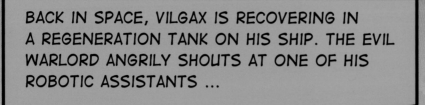

BACK IN SPACE, VILGAX IS RECOVERING IN A REGENERATION TANK ON HIS SHIP. THE EVIL WARLORD ANGRILY SHOUTS AT ONE OF HIS ROBOTIC ASSISTANTS ...

WHAT DO YOU MEAN IT'S NOT THERE? THIS BATTLE NEARLY COSTS ME MY LIFE AND YOU SAY THE OMNITRIX IS NO LONGER ON BOARD?

THE ROBOT REPORTS THAT "SENSORS INDICATE A PROBE WAS JETTISONED FROM THE SHIP JUST BEFORE BOARDING. IT LANDED ON THE PLANET BELOW."

GO!
BRING IT TO ME!

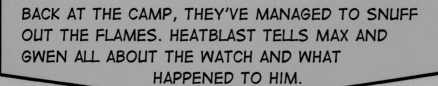

BACK AT THE CAMP, THEY'VE MANAGED TO SNUFF OUT THE FLAMES. HEATBLAST TELLS MAX AND GWEN ALL ABOUT THE WATCH AND WHAT HAPPENED TO HIM.

THINK HE'S GONNA STAY A MONSTER FOREVER?

HE'S AN ALIEN. I MEAN, LOOK AT HIM. WHAT ELSE COULD HE BE?

"I DON'T WANNA BE FIRE GUY FOREVER!"

"DON'T WORRY, BEN," SAYS MAX. "WE'LL FIGURE THIS THING OUT."

THE WATCH SUDDENLY **BLEEPS**, AND WITH A SMALL, BRIGHT EXPLOSION, HEATBLAST TURNS BACK INTO BEN!

MAX GOES TO EXPLORE THE CRATER, TELLING BEN AND GWEN TO STAY SAFE BY THE CAMP. BEN EXAMINES THE WATCH ...

"SO," SAYS GWEN, "WHAT DID IT FEEL LIKE GOING ALL ALIEN?"

IT FREAKED ME OUT AT FIRST. HEY, I THINK I FIGURED OUT HOW I DID IT. SHOULD I TRY IT AGAIN, JUST ONCE?

BEN PRESSES THE WATCH ... AND TRANSFORMS INTO A WILD-LOOKING, HAIRY, GROWLING, DROOLING BEAST. IT'S *WILDMUTT*!

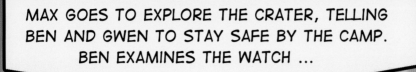

"YEUGH!" SAYS GWEN. "THIS THING'S EVEN UGLIER THAN YOU ARE NORMALLY! YOU NEED A FLEA COLLAR ON THIS MUTT! AND NO EYES? WHAT GOOD IS THIS ONE? IT CAN'T SEE!"

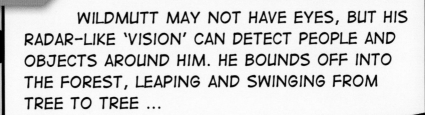

WILDMUTT MAY NOT HAVE EYES, BUT HIS RADAR-LIKE 'VISION' CAN DETECT PEOPLE AND OBJECTS AROUND HIM. HE BOUNDS OFF INTO THE FOREST, LEAPING AND SWINGING FROM TREE TO TREE ...

BEFORE LONG, WILDMUTT SENSES DANGER. A ROBOTIC DRONE FLIES TOWARDS HIM!

WILDMUTT JUMPS ON TOP OF THE DRONE. WITH HIS SHARP TEETH HE TEARS ITS WIRES OUT, AND THE DRONE SPINS WILDLY OUT OF CONTROL! WILDMUTT LEAPS OFF, SECONDS BEFORE THE MACHINE EXPLODES.

JUST THEN, WILDMUTT TURNS BACK INTO BEN. BAD TIMING! A SECOND DRONE IS HEADING STRAIGHT FOR BEN.

LUCKILY GWEN ARRIVES, AND SHE SMACKS THE DRONE HARD WITH A SPADE, AND DESTROYS IT. BEN IS IMPRESSED!

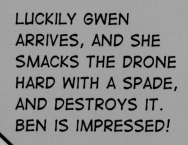

NEVER THOUGHT I'D SAY THIS, BUT AM I GLAD TO SEE YOU!

BEN AND GWEN RUN BACK TO THE CAMP TO FIND GRANDPA MAX.

BACK AT CAMP, THE TEAM HEAR A MAYDAY CALL OVER THE RUSTBUCKET'S RADIO – "MAYDAY, MAYDAY! SOMEBODY HELP US. WE'RE UNDER ATTACK BY SOME SORT OF ... ROBOT!"

SOUNDS JUST LIKE THOSE THINGS THAT ATTACKED ME, THEY MUST BE LOOKING FOR THE WATCH. I THINK I CAN HELP!

WITH A PRESS OF THE BUTTON, BEN TRANSFORMS ONCE AGAIN, THIS TIME INTO A MAN TOUGHER THAN ANY METAL. IT'S *DIAMONDHEAD!*

"SO," SAYS GWEN, "WHAT CAN THIS GUY DO?"

I DUNNO, BUT I BET IT'S GONNA BE *COOL!*

DIAMONDHEAD, MAX AND GWEN ARRIVE AT THE SCENE OF THE ATTACK. VILGAX'S HUGE ROBOTIC ASSISTANT HAS LANDED ON EARTH TO CAPTURE THE OMNITRIX. HE'S FIRING WEAPONS, CAUSING EXPLOSIONS AND FIRES. CAMPERS ARE RUNNING FOR THEIR LIVES ...

"LOOKS LIKE PAPA ROBOT THIS TIME," SAYS DIAMONDHEAD. "I'LL GET GEARHEAD'S ATTENTION. YOU TWO GUYS GET THE CAMPERS TO SAFETY."

THE ROBOT IS FIERCE, BUT DIAMONDHEAD'S GLASS-LIKE SURFACE REFLECTS ITS LASERS BACK AT IT. FINALLY, THE ROBOT RIVAL IS DESTROYED!

BACK ON HIS SPACESHIP, THE INJURED VILGAX CANNOT BELIEVE THAT HIS DRONE HAS FAILED TO GET THE OMNITRIX.

AT THE CAMPSITE, MAX AND GWEN ARE PACKING UP, GETTING READY TO LEAVE. SUDDENLY A SUPER-SPEEDY ALIEN APPEARS. IT'S BEN AS XLR8! HE ZIPS AROUND AND HELPS PACK UP THE RUSTBUCKET. HE'S SO FAST!

NO!

"I THINK THIS IS GOING TO BE THE BEST SUMMER EVER!" LAUGHS XLR8.

"ABSOLUTELY!" AGREES MAX.

"IT'S DEFINITELY GOING TO BE INTERESTING ..." SAYS GWEN.

AND THEN THERE WERE 10 QUIZ

YOU'VE READ THE STORY, NOW TEST YOUR KNOWLEDGE OF THE VERY FIRST EPISODE OF BEN 10 WITH THESE MULTIPLE CHOICE QUESTIONS!

1 WHAT IS THE NAME OF THE EVIL WARLORD WHO WANTS TO GET HIS HANDS ON THE OMNITRIX?

A) KEVIN 11 B) DR. ANIMO C) VILGAX

2 WHO IS GWEN?

A) BEN'S SISTER
B) BEN'S COUSIN
C) BEN'S BEST FRIEND

3 WHERE IS BEN WHEN WE FIRST MEET HIM?

A) IN THE RUSTBUCKET (RV)
B) IN SCHOOL
C) AT A CAMPSITE

4 WHAT IS THE FIRST MEAL THAT MAX DISHES UP FOR BEN AND GWEN?

A) MARINATED MEALWORMS
B) SMOKED FISH
C) LIVER AND BACON

5 WHAT DOES THE OMNITRIX FALL FROM?

A) AN AEROPLANE
B) VILGAX'S SPACESHIP
C) A SMALL SPACESHIP

6 WHAT IS THE NAME OF THE SECOND ALIEN THAT BEN TRANSFORMS INTO?

A) WILDMUTT
B) HEATBLAST
C) DIAMONDHEAD

7 WHAT DOES HEATBLAST ACCIDENTALLY DO?

A) FALLS INTO A CRATER
B) STARTS A FOREST FIRE
C) FLOODS THE CAMPSITE

8 WHO SAVES BEN FROM A FLYING ROBOTIC DRONE?

A) GWEN
B) MAX
C) THE OWNER OF THE CAMPSITE

9 WHY IS VILGAX IN A REGENERATION TANK?

A) HE IS TRYING TO CLONE HIMSELF
B) HE IS RECOVERING FROM HIS INJURIES
C) HE IS ASLEEP

10 WHICH ALIEN SUPERHERO HELPS TIDY UP AT THE END?

A) GHOSTFREAK
B) FOUR ARMS
C) XLR8

ANSWERS:
1-C, 2-B, 3-B, 4-A, 5-C,
6-A, 7-B, 8-A, 9-B, 10-C

ALIEN IDENTITIES

TAKE THE LETTERS SHOWN FROM THE NAMES OF EACH OF THESE ALIENS. USE THOSE LETTERS TO SPELL OUT A WORD THAT COULD BE USED TO DESCRIBE ALL OF THESE GOOD GUY ALIENS!

1 1ST LETTER

2 1ST LETTER

3 3RD LETTER

4 2ND LETTER

5 2ND LETTER

6 8TH LETTER

7 8TH LETTER

8 3RD LETTER

9 2ND LETTER

THE WORD IS:

_____ _____ _____ _____ _____ _____ _____ _____ _____
　1　　2　　3　　4　　5　　6　　7　　8　　9

VILGAX HUNT!

GREY MATTER IS LOOKING FOR VILGAX. THE RED DOT ON THE GRID BELOW SHOWS WHERE THE EVIL WARLORD WAS LAST DETECTED. FOLLOW THE INSTRUCTIONS TO FIND THE COORDINATES OF WHERE VILGAX IS NOW. USE THE COMPASS TO HELP YOU.

FROM THE RED DOT, GO:
3 SQUARES EAST
2 SQUARES NORTH
1 SQUARE WEST

ANSWER: VILGAX IS IN BLOCK C2.

THE REAL XLR8!

XLR8 IS A SUPER-SPEEDY ALIEN! HOW LONG WILL IT TAKE YOU TO SPOT THE 5 DIFFERENCES BETWEEN PICTURES 1 AND 2? ON YOUR MARKS ...

ANSWERS: XLR8 IN PICTURE 2 IS MISSING THE OMNITRIX SYMBOL, HIS RIGHT CLAW, PART OF LEFT FOOT, AND HE HAS A LARGER WHITE STRIPE ON HIS CHEST, AND AN EXTRA STRIPE ON HIS TAIL.

BEN 10 ™

THE KRAKKEN

BEN, HIS GRANDPA MAX,
AND COUSIN GWEN, ARE CAMPING BY A LAKE.
THEY SOON HEAR ABOUT A MYSTERIOUS
MONSTER OF THE DEEP ... WHAT DOES IT
WANT, AND CAN BEN'S ALIEN HEROES
HELP SAVE THE DAY?

IT'S NIGHT TIME ...
BEN'S SWIMMING IN A LAKE, SHOWING
OFF IN FRONT OF GWEN. HE SINKS
BELOW THE WATER ...

"VERY FUNNY BEN, I'M NOT FALLING FOR IT," SAYS GWEN.

SUDDENLY, A HUGE
MONSTER COVERED
IN SEAWEED REARS
UP IN FRONT OF
GWEN! **"AGGH!"** SHE
SCREAMS, AS THE
MONSTER LOOMS
OVER HER. GWEN
FALLS AND DROPS
HER TORCH.

SHE THEN REALISES
IT'S BEN AS ONE
OF HIS ALIENS –
FOUR ARMS!
"YOU ARE SO
BUSTED WHEN I
TELL GRANDPA!"

"I CAN'T BELIEVE SHE FELL FOR IT,"
LAUGHS FOUR ARMS. "A MONSTER IN THE
LAKE. HOW DUMB CAN YOU BE?"

THE NEXT MORNING, BEN AND MAX ARE GOING FISHING. GWEN DOESN'T WANT TO GO, SO SHE STAYS BEHIND ON THE PONTOON.

MAX AND BEN FIND THE BOAT THEY'VE CHARTERED AND MEET THE OWNER, A CREEPY GUY CALLED CAPTAIN SHAW.

ON THE BOAT, CAPTAIN SHAW TELLS BEN AND MAX ABOUT THE LAKE MONSTER.

IT'S CALLED THE KRAKKEN, I'VE BEEN ON ITS TAIL FOR YEARS. I COULD HELP YOU FIND THE BEAST – IF YOU'VE GOT THE STOMACH FOR A REAL ADVENTURE?

THEY MOTOR ACROSS THE LAKE TO FIND AN AREA SURROUNDED BY BUOYS, MARKED 'DO NOT ENTER'.

A BOAT COMES TOWARDS THEM, AND A MAN'S VOICE SHOUTS OUT.

STOP WHERE YOU ARE. I'M JONAH MELVILLE, THE FOUNDER OF FRIENDS OF FISH. WE'VE CLOSED THIS SECTION OF THE LAKE FOR AN ENVIRONMENTAL STUDY. YOU'LL HAVE TO TURN AROUND.

BUT WHAT ABOUT THE KRAKKEN?

"HA HA, THE KRAKKEN?" JONAH LAUGHS. "NOT THAT OLD FISH STORY. LOOK, I'M A MARINE BIOLOGIST, AND ANYBODY WHO TELLS YOU THEY'VE SEEN A MONSTER IN THIS LAKE IS CASTING WITHOUT A HOOK."

SUDDENLY, THE SONAR ON SHAW'S BOAT STARTS BLEEPING ...

THE SONAR! WE'VE FOUND SOMETHING!

OR SOMETHING'S FOUND US, *LOOK!*

THE LAKE GETS ROUGHER AND ROUGHER UNTIL A MONSTER APPEARS! IT'S *THE KRAKKEN* AND IT'S HEADING STRAIGHT FOR THE PONTOON – AND ALL THE TOURISTS! THE KRAKKEN REARS UP, DWARFING EVERYBODY. IT CRASHES INTO THE PONTOON AND SWEEPS GWEN INTO THE WATER!

TIME TO GO HERO! BEN PRESSES THE OMNITRIX, HOPING FOR RIPJAWS, THE UNDERWATER ALIEN. BUT XLR8 APPEARS INSTEAD!

XLR8 LEAPS ON BOARD JONAH'S BOAT. THE KRAKKEN IS TRYING TO PULL A WOODEN CRATE OUT OF JONAH'S HANDS. BUT XLR8 FIGHTS OFF THE LAKE MONSTER, AND SAVES THE CRATE!

WHAT'S SO IMPORTANT IN THAT CRATE THAT YOU RISKED YOUR LIFE FOR IT?

EH, OUR LUNCH.

XLR8 CAN'T BELIEVE IT. "YOU ALMOST GOT MUNCHED FOR A FEW SANDWICHES?" HE ASKS.

THE KRAKKEN GRABS THE CRATE AGAIN. XLR8 CHASES IT ACROSS THE LAKE, BUT THE OMNITRIX STARTS BLEEPING ... AND XLR8 TURNS BACK INTO A VERY WET BEN!

BACK ON THE SURFACE, SHAW FINDS THREE MYSTERIOUS, MASKED MEN ON HIS BOAT.

I HAVEN'T ANYTHING WORTH STEALING.

AH, BUT YOU HAVE US ALL WRONG, ALL WE WANT IS SOME INFORMATION. LIKE WHAT DID YOU SEE DOWN THERE?

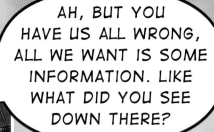

"NOTHING," SAYS SHAW. "SAME AS ALWAYS."

SMACK! THE MAN HITS SHAW IN THE FACE, KNOCKING HIM UNCONSCIOUS. THE MAN PULLS OFF HIS MASK. IT'S JONAH!

STILL IN THE LAKE, BEN HAS SEEN AND HEARD EVERYTHING. HE PRESSES DOWN ON HIS WATCH. IT DOESN'T WORK!

STINKFLY IS GROUNDED – HIS WINGS ARE TOO WET FOR TAKEOFF!

THINKING QUICKLY, STINKFLY SHOOTS SOME GREEN SLIME FROM HIS POLLEN DUCTS, AND USES IT TO SWING HIMSELF UP INTO A TREE!

HE SPOTS JONAH DUMPING CAPTAIN SHAW OVERBOARD ...

... AND SPEEDS DOWN TO PLUCK SHAW FROM THE LAKE AND BACK UP INTO THE AIR!

SHAW STILL WANTS TO CAPTURE THE KRAKKEN! MAX, BEN AND GWEN SPEED OFF FOR THE CANNERY, LEAVING SHAW STRANDED AT THE DOCKS.

AT THE CANNERY, JONAH IS HELPING TO LIFT EGGS OUT OF THE LAKE.

CAREFUL, OR YOU'LL BE CLEANING UP THE WORLD'S MOST EXPENSIVE OMELETTE. AFTER WE SELL THESE BABIES, WE'LL BE KICKING BACK ON A BEACH IN THE BAHAMAS!

THE GANG ARRIVE AT THE CANNERY. BEN DECIDES IT'S TIME TO KICK SOME FRIENDS OF FISH TAIL! HE PRESSES DOWN ON THE OMNITRIX AND BECOMES ...

RIPJAWS!

AT LAST, RIPJAWS SNATCHES THE PRECIOUS EGGS FROM JONAH, AND GENTLY PLACES THEM AT THE BOTTOM OF THE LAKE.

JONAH IS CAUGHT BY THE KRAKKEN WHO CRUNCHES HIS ARMED SUBMARINE BETWEEN HER RAZOR-SHARP TEETH, AND DESTROYS IT.

THE KRAKKEN IS ABOUT TO GOBBLE JONAH UP ... BUT RIPJAWS GETS BETWEEN THEM BOTH.

THE KRAKKEN RETURNS TO HER EGGS AND NEST. MEANWHILE, RIPJAWS SWINGS ROUND, AND *SMACKS* JONAH IN THE FACE. THE DUDE'S OUT COLD!